A CAPTAIN'S ORDER

Scandalous London Series

TAMARA GILL

A Captain's Order
Scandalous London Series
Novella Two

Copyright 2015 by Tamara Gill
Cover Art by EDH Graphics

ISBN-13: 9781973267621

DEDICATION

For anyone who loves a little scandal…

CHAPTER 1

Colony of New South Wales, 1810

E loise sponged her brother's brow and still he twisted and turned with a fever that wouldn't abate. The doctor she'd summoned the night before, after Andrew had fallen ill at dinner, called it a fever brought on from an insect bite.

She swallowed hard and refused to believe the statistic he'd dealt her. All those he'd nursed had died. It wasn't fathomable. "Andrew, try and drink a little." She lifted his head and he moaned an awful sound that reeked of death.

Her vision of him blurred. She couldn't lose her brother. Not so young. Not here. He should be home raising hell in the ballrooms of the ton, not dying an awful death half way around the world with little or no amenities to help him.

"Fetch the doctor again. He's getting worse." Eloise managed to get a little moisture between his lips before he started to shake uncontrollably. His face was red, blotchy with heat, and yet he moaned he was cold.

She prayed to god that should this be his end that it would come quickly. A good, kind soul didn't deserve to die in such heinous conditions. "Andrew darling, talk to me. Tell me what to do."

He didn't answer, his breathing ragged then laboured. Panic clawed at her throat that he wouldn't see another sunrise. Oh dear god, she couldn't be left alone. He was all she had left. "Please, dearest. Please try."

The bedroom door slammed open and Dr Jones walked briskly to her brother's side. He checked him over, his heart, listened to his breathing, noted his eyes and stood back, a consoling, pitying face she didn't want to see.

"I'm sorry Lady Eloise, but your brother will not make it. He's showing all the signs that I have noted before with this disease. We will try and keep him as comfortable for as long as possible, but you must prepare yourself."

A blackness threatened to consume her. "Prepare myself? Are you delusional! I don't care what you have to do, but you can't let my brother die. Now search through that bag of yours you carry about and pull out a miracle."

He patted her hand that lay over Andrew's brow. "I'm not being intentionally cruel, my lady. Your brother is dying. I'm sorry."

She shook her head not wanting to acknowledge the truth of the words. And unfortunately, Andrew did pass and her brother was no longer.

A few hours later, Eloise sat beneath the veranda of the Governor of New South Wales' home in Sydney town wondering how she'd come to be an orphan. Because that was, exactly what she was now. A woman of independent means in the most awful of ways.

She would have to return home to England and soon. The trip she'd looked forward to with her brother was no longer viable or wanted. This country was hard, hot and somewhere she'd always associate with grief.

Yes. It was definitely time to go home.

"Captain. Please, I will pay double for the fare back to England, or however far you can take me."

The man looked at her as if she were daft. And maybe she was. Her voice certainly had an desperate edge even she cringed at hearing.

"We're full. You'll need to find another vessel." He turned his back on her and started to shout out orders to his men.

"The ship I sailed here on left last week. There isn't another one for months and I must return home. I have no family left here. I'll sleep on deck if I have to, just give me passage. Please, I'm begging you."

He sighed and ran a hand through his hair. His stance one of annoyance. He turned and took in her appearance. "Fine, but you'll pay double and the only place for you to sleep is in a small closet that runs beside my room. I doubt sleeping in with the crew would be wise." He nodded toward her luggage. "Are they your bags?"

"Yes. I didn't bring a lot as I thought to have clothing made here to suit the climate. And well…"

He held up his hands. "Spare me the details. Come aboard." He yelled out to one of his crewmen who jogged over to them. "Take…ahh." He gestured toward her. "I'm sorry, I don't know your name."

"Oh, of course I should have said. I apologize. I'm Lady Eloise Bartholomew."

The captain raised his brow and a pained expression crossed his features. "Take Lady Bartholomew to my cabin and clear out the stores room beside my room, put a cot in there for her. And Hamish, make sure the crew know she's off limits."

Eloise felt her eyes widen at the captain's words. *Off limits*. What did that mean? Had she inadvertently placed herself in more danger here than on the mainland with animals and insects that could kill you within hours? "Thank you," she said as she followed the other man. The captain walked off without another word and busied himself on deck, obviously busy with getting the ship ready for sail.

She wished she were returning home on better circumstances, but she was not. Only after a few weeks of arriving here, she was about to embark on another six month journey across the seas.

She groaned. How would she ever bear it...

CHAPTER 2

Six months later off the coast of England, 1811

The sea ebbed and flowed around her; great waves rolled and brought her ever closer to home. Yet never had Eloise felt more homeless.

England.

So different from the dry, barren, and barely civilized colony of New South Wales. Six months it had taken them to travel there, on a brother's whim to visit new climes and enjoy his newly acquired inheritance. An inheritance now solely hers because of his sudden death to a fever they blamed on a mosquito.

Eloise shook her head at the knowledge such an insignificant bug could kill a man in his prime. A much-loved brother left on foreign shores many miles from where he, the earl, should have been laid to rest at Belmont House, Surrey.

They docked not an hour later in the murky brown water of the Thames. The filthy stench from the overpopulated waterway made her yearn for the crystal streams that surrounded Sydney Town.

"Right this way, m'lady, if you please." No doubt, years of wind and sea had hardened the gravelly voice of the man stepping around her.

Eloise followed the hunched gentleman off the boat and walked toward a highly polished, enclosed carriage. Dark and foreboding, it reeked of her future.

That of a lady. With a title she no longer deserved . . . .

Because the daughter of an earl did not yearn for the touch of a hardened sea captain. Nor desire, nor crave, his roughened, stubble-strewn jaw marring the skin of her most intimate places.

And yet she did. Desperately.

Before she was three feet from the vehicle, the door opened with a snap, and a childhood friend, now woman, alighted—ribbons and frills flying about her like a kite in strong winds—pulling Eloise from her troubled thoughts.

She laughed. "Emma." She hugged her dearest friend, the overpowering smell of rosewater making her eyes water. "I have missed you."

"You are home. Oh, dearest, England has been such a bore without you. How have you been? You must tell me of your voyage and all you know of this wild land you have visited. I long to travel and would visit such a place if my Bertie would allow. But"—Emma rubbed the distinctive lump under her skirt—"because of my current condition I am not allowed."

Eloise smiled, biting back the nip of jealousy over her friend's happy news. "Congratulations. I'm happy for you and Lord Rine. And as soon as I'm home and settled, I promise to tell you all."

Well, perhaps not all. How could she explain the Lady Eloise Bartholomew had fallen in love? Lain with a man out of wedlock and enjoyed every decadent, sinful moment of it.

Deep in her belly, a thread of desire thrummed at the thought of his hands. His lips, grazing her skin, kissing her breasts, her—

"Are you well, Eloise? You look flushed." Emma frowned. "Oh dear, I do hope you are not falling ill, my dear."

"I'm perfectly well, I—"

"I heard of Andrew's demise." Emma clasped her hand. "I'm so sorry, dearest, truly sorry. He was a wonderful man, whose life was cut tragically short. I wish I had been there for you."

Eloise blinked, refusing to give in to emotions already running high. "Thank you. I wish you had been there as well."

"Come," Emma said. "Let's get you home."

Eloise settled her skirts on the leather squabs, the excess material feeling bulky and awkward around her legs. For months, while on the ship home, she had worn breeches, shirts, and a jacket to keep her modest when in the view of the captain's crew. The freedom had been liberating for a girl used to the strictures of society. After the death of her brother, something inside her snapped.

No longer was she willing to pass through life unhappy, doing what everyone else thought was right. For, within a moment of time, one's life could be over. And she'd lived by the rule for six months. But her hiatus of freedom had now ended. She was an aristocrat, and with such dire circumstances came the dreaded high-waisted gowns of English fashion, and responsibilities she now had to face.

"Tell me," she said, changing the subject. "Everything I have missed while I was away. What's the latest on dit scandalising the ton?"

Eloise listened to her friend's gossip and exploits covering the last fifteen months, but sadly, she had heard it all before. Life, it seemed, did not change in London during the season or at the ton's country homes during the winter. As usual, life here was tedious to the extreme.

And the complete opposite of what she had tasted.

CHAPTER 3

Somewhere between the colony of New South Wales and England, 1810

Gabe sat on a wooden water barrel and watched as Eloise tried to learn the art of tying knots with his second in command, Hamish Doherty. He laughed to himself at the irony of the situation. For the last two month's that's exactly what she'd been doing to him. Tying him in knots.

With a will of their own, his eyes took in her summery gown, the gentle breeze giving him a view of her lovely ankles every now and then. Her attire wasn't appropriate for this type of voyage and he really ought to supply her with some breeches and shirts.

He swallowed as the vision of what she'd look like in such attire flooded his mind like a rogue wave. All her delicious curves would be there for him to admire. The roundness of her bottom, a lovely handful he'd ache to clasp. The thinness of her waist accentuated by breasts that were lovely and pert.

Oh dear lord. He was turning into a perverted fiend.

Eloise laughed at something Hamish said and a twinge of jealousy shot through him. He stood and walked over to them before picking up his own slip of rope and sitting.

Hamish nodded and stood. "I have things to do, Lady Eloise. I'll leave you with the good captain to carry on our lesson."

"Thank you, Hamish."

She didn't meet his eye, only seemed to concentrate more on the knot she was learning.

"Do you need some help?"

Eloise pulled the rope from her hand, a muffled curse escaping from her lips. "It's supposed to be a stopper knot. I can't seem to thread the rope right."

Gabe moved to sit beside her and took her hand. Her skin was soft, warm and made his flesh sizzle with desire. He felt the rate of his heart increase at the close proximity to her. Taking a deep breath, he rallied himself to calm down. It was only a knot after all.

"You must with this knot hold your hand solidly in this way. The rope will then thread and link more easily for you. Here," he said, picking up his discarded rope. "Let me show you."

He quickly finished and held it out for her to review. She smiled, laughing he mused at her own inability before trying again. Again he helped her to ensure her hand remained solidly fixed in one position and with a couple of tries she pulled the stopper knot into the form it should be.

"I did it!" She stood and waved it at Hamish now manning the wheel. "Look Hamish. The knot."

He nodded. "Well done, my lady. I knew Captain Lyons would teach you well."

"Thank you." She sat, staring at him and again he was left breathless at the innocent beauty of her features. No rouge sullied her complexion; she was as natural as the elements around them. Perhaps even more beautiful. "I've never accomplished anything like that before. My hobbies are usually limited to needle work or drawing."

"Both amiable qualities, but out here, it's always helpful to have other skills." He pulled her to stand and started to walk toward his cabin. "Talking of practicability, your attire is probably not the most comfortable on board a ship like mine. I hope you don't think me impertinent, but maybe you'd like to wear breeches and shirts instead of gowns. I think I have some clothing packed away that would fit you."

Her emerald eyes sparkled like gems in the sun. "That would be wonderful. I would love that."

He led her downstairs to his cabin and bade her welcome to his room. He'd been steadfast in keeping her out of this space. Just the thought of what they could do together, enjoy together in a bed that mocked him almost physically hurt.

It was easy throwing a few clothing items together and if he looked rushed it was because he was. The sooner she left the better.

"These should fit. You can change in here if you like and come up on deck."

She walked up to him and took the clothing from his hands. Eloise caught his gaze and a question lurked beneath her long eyelashes and one he ached she'd ask. "Why have you never tried to kiss me, Captain Lyons? I've caught you watching me and yet you never even once try and see if your desire is reciprocated."

Gabe leaned against the dresser with an air of nonchalance that was a total farce. "Do many men try and kiss you, Lady Eloise?"

"Just Eloise, please. I think our circumstances and location warrant the loosening of society's rules." She grinned. "As to your question I will not deny that I've been approached on more than one occasion for a stolen moment or two."

"Really." He tried to shake the building anger that other men had tasted her lips. Clasped her delectable body against theirs and taken her mouth in an embrace that would beckon them for more forever. "Are you so in demand?"

She shrugged. "I am an Earl's daughter and now that my brother's gone it is time I secured my future and married."

Sadness flickered through her gaze and Gabe wanted nothing but to go to her, pull her against himself and hold her. "Is that what you really want?" Something told him it wasn't. To ask such a forward question as to why he hadn't kissed her only meant one thing. Maybe she wanted him too.

Gabe closed the space between them and looked down, waited for her to meet his gaze. His body thrummed with suppressed desire. Every impulse in his body wanted to devour, take, conquer and enjoy, but he couldn't. "Have you ever been really kissed, my lady? Kissed to within an inch of your sanity, like your body is burning and needing the person in your arms as much as the air you breathe?"

She licked her lips and he bit back a groan. "I've never been kissed like that."

"I want to kiss you like that."

Eloise nodded, her eyes wide with wonder. "You do?"

"Oh yes, I most certainly do." And he did. No sooner had the words left his body did his mouth fuse with hers. Never had he felt such soft lips. Lips that copied each of his movements like a mirror image. Gabe swept his tongue across hers as he pulled her hard against his chest.

She fit him like a perfectly made kid leather glove. Her breasts pressed against his body and through her gown he could feel her nipples bead with desire. Her breathing hitched as he plundered her mouth, sank deeper and pulled her further into the world he desperately wanted her to seek.

He wanted her. His cock strained against his pants and, rogue ship captain that he was, he ground himself against her sex. She gasped, her eyes going wide at the unfamiliar touch, but still she didn't pull away. Instead, her arms came about his neck as she lifted herself to fit against him more snugly.

Gabe groaned and continued to kiss her. Without heed, or support they stood in the centre of his cabin, locked within each other's arms, their mouths locked in an endless battle of need.

Eloise gasped and he knew what their bodies were doing to one another was making her hot, exciting her and bringing her closer to release. He could make her come fully clothed and the thought itself was enough to confirm his plans.

He ran his hand over her bottom and clasped her high on her leg, lifting her and placing her directly against his heat. Her fingers clenched his hair as a slight blush rose on her cheeks.

She was close, so tantalizing close, but not there yet. He supposed he could lay her over his desk, throw up her skirts and lick her to fulfilment. But not yet, he doubted she would be ready to go that far…yet.

Instead he made certain her sex was being teased in exactly the right location. Over and over again he fucked her little bud with his cock, teasing her, making her want more.

Eloise didn't disappoint. "Yes. Oh yes." Her breathy

words sent fire to his groin just as she hugged him as her orgasm took hold. Gabe continued to dry fuck her as the last of her shuddering subsided. His cock ached for release and he shook away his need.

There was plenty of months left on this ship left yet.

He took her lips in a quick kiss. "Do you like my kisses?" He grinned.

"Your kisses are exemplary, and they have more than satisfied me, Captain Lyons."

He pushed a lock of hair from her face and marvelled at her beauty. "I always strive to keep my passengers happy. A captain's duty."

She laughed. "And a passengers fortune."

CHAPTER 4

London, 1811

Eloise stood in a gilded ballroom in the home of her dearest friend. The surprise celebration marked her return to England and to society. But the crush, intoxicating smells, and the deafening volume of the entertainment overwhelmed her senses.

Although she pasted on a smile, nodded, and spoke at the appropriate times, her heart was no longer in this life. The satins and jewels held no interest. The men in their finely cut suits did not stir her desire nor engender thoughts of futures together.

Nothing.

Only one man sat in her thoughts, and yet, he should not. For had she not left him in Africa? His home. Or so he had told her when he refused to travel the rest of the distance to England to be with her.

Marry her.

"Darling, there is someone who wishes to meet you."

Emma dragged her toward the opposite end of the room. "He's very handsome and just perfect for you."

Eloise bit back a resigned sigh. She should move on with her life, find a husband to take care of her. Love her, just as she'd planned. "Emma, I do not wish . . . that is to say—" She paused when the gentleman in question came into view. Oh dear, he was handsome if one could ignore the excessively starched shirt collar he sported. Eloise curtsied and allowed Lord Rine to introduce her to Lord Daniel Fenshaw, a baron from Norfolk.

The gentleman looked to be in his early thirties if the smile lines about his eyes were any indication. With an athletic build, he towered over her, and made her modest height seem small and delicate. But something in his eyes gave her pause and tempered her response to his ardent words and charm.

"I understand you have recently arrived back from the colonies. The land, I hear, if one could live without niceties, is quite beautiful."

"Yes, it is," Eloise said. "Although I didn't venture to the bush, I did see many beautiful sights. The plants and their flowers are unlike any I've known, and the creeks and rivers run with the clearest water I've ever seen."

"Sounds like you miss it."

She paused and wondered if such a notion was true. "I was not there long as my brother fell ill only a week or so after arriving. I don't miss anything of the country other than my brother who is buried there." Perhaps that wasn't quite true. The freedom she'd enjoyed there would forever make the strictures of this life fray her patience. Her trip home had been just as wonderful and enjoyable. Not to mention . . . pleasurable.

The captain.

A man whom she watched, awestruck, when he

climbed the tall masts and rigging. Steered the pitching ship through choppy waters determined to capture the vessel for itself and submerge it in a watery grave. Only after two months she was pleased to call him her friend and often times her only confidant. She'd hidden her growing lust for him until, unable to stand the situation any longer, she'd taken a chance and seduced him...

The day in their cabin when he'd first made her orgasm, fully clothed and in the middle of the day would be a memory she'd cherish forever.

Eloise snatched a glass of champagne from a passing waiter. "The country will forever hold a place in my memories, but I doubt I will see it again. Dreadfully long voyage, you understand." She smiled as she met Lord Fenshaw's gaze, hoping her blasé tone would end the conversation.

"Yes, Lady Rine mentioned you travelled back via a merchant ship to Africa, then caught the Oriental from there." He paused and smiled to a passing acquaintance. "What was the name of the boat you travelled to Africa on, if you recall?"

Eloise frowned, and a tingle of unease prickled her skin. "Ah, I believe the ship was called Esperance, my lord."

He nodded but said nothing; instead, he looked out over the throng of guests milling around them. Eloise searched for Emma, meaning to slip away and join her, when his lordship turned to her with an intense, probing stare. She shifted her feet, unease creeping down her spine from the awkward silence that settled like a dark cloud over them.

"Six months is a long time for a lady to be at sea. Alone." The gentleman cleared his throat as if thinking better of what he was about to say. "I was saddened to hear of your brother's death. He was an honourable man."

Eloise looked down at her drink and blinked, refusing to give way to more tears, a most inappropriate reaction, which came upon her when people spoke of Andrew. "Thank you, my lord. That is very kind."

"Are you attending the masquerade ball at Lord Durham's on Saturday?"

A smile quirked her lips when she noted Emma making her way across the room to her. "I am. 'Tis an event I've been told not to miss."

He smiled in response. "It's an event I would not want you to miss, Lady Eloise." Holding her gaze, he bowed before taking his leave. Eloise watched him go, and the unease that prickled her skin before now stabbed. She turned to Emma, wondering why his smile had not reached his eyes. Insincere, as if he knew something she did not.

Not yet at least.

CHAPTER 5

"So, dearest, what do you think of Lord Fenshaw? Isn't he the most fabulous man?"

"Oh, very much so." Eloise fought the urge to roll her eyes at her friend's absurd notion. "From memory, his sister came out the same year we did. Has she married?"

Emma's face clouded with sadness, and she wondered at it. "Yes, Miss Fenshaw. A beautiful woman, if not a little flighty and rebellious."

"There is nothing wrong with a woman wanting independence." Eloise regretted the sharp edge to her tone as soon as she'd said it. She sighed. "I apologise, I did not mean to snap."

Emma clasped her arm. "Independence is all very well, but at what price? I believe Miss Fenshaw paid dearly for hers."

Eloise met her friend's gaze. "What do you mean?"

They walked toward the supper room and away from the crowded ballroom. "I do not know all the particulars, but what I do know is her brother, unable to control her bizarre and promiscuous behaviour, institutionalised the woman. You see, she kept running away. From what I know, she died three years ago in childbirth at the hospital. Rumour would lead you to believe Miss Fenshaw also tried to harm herself while living there. A terrible sickness the family couldn't cure with love and help." Emma paused. "Lord Fenshaw loved her dearly and was understandably devastated by the loss of his sister. But the exact, under-lying cause of her demise and condition has never been known."

"How do you know this?" Eloise asked.

Emma leaned in closer to her. "I should not. No one should. Lord Fenshaw's family tried to hush up the fact his sister was a lunatic, but . . . servants do talk."

"Oh, how dreadful for them all, and poor Miss Fenshaw, she seemed such a lively and popular girl." Eloise sat at a table for two and welcomed the footman who brought over a fresh glass of champagne. Looking at her friend's morose visage, she set about changing the subject. "What are you wearing to the Masquerade?"

"I thought I should go as a Venetian courtesan. Bertie wishes to go as himself. Such a bore, don't you agree?"

Eloise laughed. "Not a bore, just being himself, I suppose. I'm not sure what I wish to go as." She shrugged. "I'll think of something."

"Well," Emma said, biting into a crab cake, leaving a little amount of dipping sauce on her chin. "You will want to think fast. The ball of the season is only two days away."

Eloise motioned to her friend's chin, then laughed when Emma's complexion turned as red as the lobster shell she now held.

. . .

Gabriel Lyons, more formally known as, His Grace the Duke of Dale, narrowed his eyes at the buildings and magnificent townhouses gracing his square in Mayfair. For the tenth time that day, he wondered if he should call out to his midshipmen and order them back to the docks. Back to his ship and back to Africa. Return to a home, which, no matter how geographically distant, would always be a more welcoming sight than the one before him. To think, he, the Duke of Dale, chased the skirts of a recalcitrant Lady Eloise Bartholomew hundreds of miles, was an illogical notion. Yet, when his carriage pulled before his stately Georgian mansion, and his door opened, within a moment, he knew such a thing was indeed true.

Fool.

Gabe looked up with loathing at the Corinthian columns gracing his front door and inwardly cursed at his elder brother's inability to stay alive. With heavy feet wanting to drag him back to the docks, he walked up the steps. Always a man to allow his wilder side little-to-no restraint, Gabe despised the fact he needed to pick up the title of duke—and all the obligations and strictures with that title. The mere thought did not sit well with his restless soul.

A soul that yearned for the swell of the ocean, the smooth wood of the ships wheel, and sails billowing with the gift of wind on an endless ocean. Sand beneath his feet with every new and unexplored destination, many of which he had still to venture. And perhaps now, never would.

Gabe sighed. Here he was about to cause one of the biggest upsets in the ton in years with his return and his proposal to a woman who'd tamed his heart.

To a point.

He walked into his library and slumped behind his desk, clean of papers. Gabe made a mental note to thank his steward, who looked after all his estates in his absence. Laying his head back, he stared up at the ornate ceiling depicting cherubs and women, lying on silks, surrounded by fruit and flowers of every kind, and he thought of Eloise.

Their parting had not gone well…

The ship had sailed toward Cape Town, where the mountains behind the city peeked over the waves on the horizon. Gabe handed back the looking glass to Hamish Doherty, his midshipman, aware a part of him wished he could delay their landing. But he could not. The men were restless for the pleasures only land could afford. Women, and the services they provided, food, and a bed that did not sway were paramount in their minds. He could not delay any longer.

His lips quirked when feminine arms came about his waist, followed by a warm, lithe body against his back. Gabe clasped her hands and pulled her tighter against him. "Awake already? Did I not wear you out sufficiently enough last night?"

A chuckle against his back, followed by a kiss, fired blood directly to his groin. "I feel so alive and invigorated. I couldn't possibly sleep a moment longer. Even if the temptation to sleep in your bed is so very great."

Gabe turned and pulled her against him, allowed his hand to flex the globe of her arse. "Perhaps we should go below decks."

Eloise's lips took his, and once more, he was lost. Lost at sea in the arms of a woman whose innocence he had seductively taken. He savoured the delectable lips and met her thrust of tongue with his own, pulled away only when she started to rub against him like a purring cat.

"You do realise we are being watched," he said.

She stilled in his arms and looked over her shoulder. Gabe laughed at the unladylike curse from her lips. It seemed he was a bad influence on her.

"Perhaps it would be best, Captain, if we went below. I do believe I am in further need of your services."

"Is that an order?" he asked, pulling her toward the stairway, ignoring the catcalls following their every step.

"Yes."

Gabe stepped off the last step in the corridor below. At the saucy look she threw him, he lost his equanimity. He pushed her against the wooden wall and took her lips in a punishing kiss. Allowed his hard and ready body to undulate against her, brought a whimper to her lips that fuelled his raw need to take her.

Eloise lifted one leg and wrapped it against his hip, her hot core burning him through her breeches. Gabe released a hungry growl and clasped her delicate thigh, cursing her attire and wishing she wore a skirt for easier access. A quicker fuck.

Still, there were other ways around the predicament.

He slipped his hands from her and caught the buttons keeping him at bay. Every one popped and sprinkled to the floor; he ignored her startled gasp and knowing smile and shoved her pants down.

"No undergarments. A woman after my own heart." His heart thumped as he devoured the delicious, rumpled sight she made— rosy cheeks, eyes glazed, and body bare from the waist down.

"After your heart, Captain? I already own it."

Gabe met her eyes and took her lips in a searing kiss, welcomed her frantic fingers against his breeches, shivered when she pushed them down his hips and clasped his arse.

She was a wanton. His wanton.

Beyond caring where they were, Gabe lifted her and moaned when his rod slid easily into her wet heat. Eloise's hot core clasped tight about him as he pumped into her, the slap of the waves against the boat and the slap of skin all he could hear.

Her tight passage pulled at him in ways he'd never thought possible. Eloise had a beautiful soul, one he should have left alone, yet she tempted like a siren, a goddess of the sea, and he had not been able to walk away from the fire she ignited in him.

He'd wanted her from the first. And had taken her when the opportunity had arisen, the day Eloise had asked him to make love to her. The memory shot blood to his groin.

Like now, begging for him not to stop, and Gabe, unable to deny her anything, followed her command. The creamy, soft skin smelling of lavender intoxicated his senses.

And he was lost...

She threw back her head and moaned as their bodies continued to mate with a frenzied need. Heedless of their location he pumped into her relentlessly, wanting to feel her body clamp tight about him, quiver up his shaft and pull him into his own orgasmic pleasure.

"Yes. Like that."

He adjusted his hold to pull her legs higher about his waist. She gasped and he knew she was close. Little mewling sounds puffed out with each expelled breath and then she came. He kissed the scream from her lips, dragged her sensual tongue into his mouth and kissed her until his own release followed. Fuck this woman had him in knots. She held him captive and it suited him more than he'd ever admit.

"Your Grace, dinner is served."

Gabe opened his eyes with a careless nonchalance he did not feel. Inside, his body burned for her. Needed her, like a Clipper needed water to sail the high seas.

"Thank you." He watched the elderly retainer, in service since his father's time, hobble from the room. He adjusted his rod, hard and beyond uncomfortable, in his pants and wondered where Eloise was at this moment.

At a ball? Dancing? With another man…

He stood and walked toward the dining room, determined to have a quick bite and some after-dinner entertainment. Entertainment that would include his future bride.

CHAPTER 6

Eloise stood at the terrace doors and looked over the sea of unrecognisable heads at the masquerade ball. The ton had gone to extreme costs dressing up as courtesans, pirates, Venetians, gods and monks.

A smile quirked her lips when a man dressed as a wolf stalked his prey, the woman not at all fazed by such pursuit but indifferent and even a little annoyed. She sighed and watched Lord Rine and Emma waltz around the floor. They made a beautiful couple, obviously, very much in love.

Eloise beat down the loneliness she had come to accept these past weeks. It wasn't her fault Gabe had pushed her away. She had spoken up and asked for what she wanted. Him. His refusal was of his own choosing and nothing more she could have said or done would have changed his mind. A man not used to the strictures of having a woman about and what that would mean for his bachelor life.

Pigheaded captain. She adjusted her black mask to sit correctly on her nose, wishing to remain anonymous. The only part of her face people could see were her lips, painted a deep red this eve, the opposite of the natural look she normally sported when at balls and parties. Dressed as Galatea, a goddess of the sea, Eloise felt seductive and beautiful for the first time in an age. Emma had sewn a small dolphin for her to hold, and the gown she wore poured over her like water and looked just as transparent in some light.

Not that she expected anyone to guess who she was. But tonight was for fun, and she was determined to have some. She needed to keep her mind off a certain man who haunted her every dream and every waking hour.

Gabe.

"May I have this dance?" The rich baritone ran through her and left her short of breath. She looked at the man bowing before her and frowned. There was something...

The dark hair behind his full-face mask gave him away, not to mention the eyes, deep pools of blue that spoke of sinful nights and weeks of longing.

But it couldn't be. He was in Cape Town. Thousands of miles away.

"Gabe?"

He pulled her into his arms and swung her into the throng of dancers. "Ah, so my goddess of the sea knows who I am."

Eloise's knees threatened to collapse, and as if he sensed her shock, he placed his hand about her back and held her fast. The hint of ocean emanated from him, dragging her under a wave of feelings only the blackguard before her could raise. A man who'd allowed her to sail into the sunset without so much as a by-your-leave. And yet, when he looked at her like he was now, with hungry eyes and lips lifted in a sensual smirk that made her stomach clench, it was so very hard to stay angry at him.

She cleared her throat. "I'm amazed a ship captain would know mythological history?"

His lips quirked, and so too did her pulse. "I'm well versed in many things." The seductive glint in his eyes left her with no misunderstanding of his meaning, and Eloise ignored the desire that shot through her at being so close to him again. Ignored his thighs as they grazed against her skirts, reminding her of the fact he had allowed her to leave. Perhaps marry another. She looked over his shoulder, the pain of his abandonment a torment still.

Had he even cared for her at all? They had made love so many times that eventually she lost count. Was she only used for his satisfaction, a plaything to while away the many months at sea? He'd always been honest as to where he called home, and eventually they had docked in Cape Town, but what had happened next had been something she'd never even contemplated.

At first the chance to see an unknown land lifted her spirits higher than they already soared...until Gabe had explained he would not be accompanying her to England. Would in fact, be staying in Africa for the foreseeable future. Without her.

Just the memory made the bottom of her soul drop to the floor with a thump, as if an anchor had been heaved at her, splitting her heart in two.

"Hard to forget the man who left me." She quickly met his gaze, her own narrowing. "What are you doing here? I did not think you cared for England or anyone who lived there."

The arms about her waist pulled her closer than she should allow, and her body, remembering every decadent thing they had ever done, purred silently with the contact.

"You left me if I recall correctly. You must know I

could never forget you." His breath whispered against her ear sent shivers of desire along her spine.

Eloise moaned and allowed her hand about his waist to venture under his domino, allowed him to see what his touch did to her. Fired her blood and made her crave a secluded corner so they could be alone.

Then in a voice that belied her actions, she said, "Oh, but did you not say the last time we spoke, you would rather die than step foot in the cesspit they call England. That, and I quote, 'not even my delectable rump would change your mind'."

She quirked an eyebrow at the resounding chuckle.

"Forgive me, my lady, I was not myself. The thought of you leaving…well, shall we just say I did not take it well."

Eloise snorted. "You couldn't wait to be rid of me. After everything we had been through you couldn't even bother to see me off. Do not stand here and spout foolish words you do not mean." She stepped back and curtsied. "Have a pleasant evening, Captain. Oh, and a pleasant life, preferably one back in the Africa you are so fond of."

Considering the fury she noted behind his mask at her words, Eloise was surprised she made the corridor running adjacent to the ballroom before a large, voyage-roughened hand clasped her arm and pulled her to a stop.

"You know I never meant anything I said that day. I was upset. You were leaving me. Refused"—he pointed a finger at her nose—"to stay and live with me away from this life you once loved."

"Still love," she said, knowing she had never spoken such an untruth in her life.

Eloise noted the muscle in his jaw work while he digested her falsehood. Fear, unlike any she had ever known, assailed her when he let go and stood back, his eyes devoid of any emotion. "Forgive me. It seems I have been mistaken. I will leave you now. Goodnight."

A moment of panic left her stunned. She didn't want him to leave, just to punish him a little for leaving her broken hearted. Foolish bounder.

"You step back into that ballroom, Gabe, and you will never step a foot near me again."

A smile quirked his lips, which he smoothed before turning to face the wicked woman he loved more than any foreign country, ship, or the abundant wealth he had inherited. "Is that a threat?"

She turned and walked up the corridor before opening a door and disappearing into a room. Gabe looked along the passage and, noting its desertion, followed. Snipped the lock shut when he entered, and leant against the cool, wooden door at his back.

"You wished to say something, my lady?" He fought the urge to smile at her upturned, defiant little chin. He bit his lip lest he close the distance between them and nip at it until she begged for forgiveness or more. He'd take either.

"What are you doing here? How did you get an invite?"

"Ah." Gabe sat on a nearby chair and met her curious stare. "I was invited." "Really." Her mocking gaze indicated she did not believe his words for the truth they were. "You are saying, Captain Lyons, Lord Durham invited a terror of the seas, a man who has fleeced many an English ship, to his ball?"

He shrugged. "I did not fleece. It was always paid work. But your answer is yes."

"Why?"

Gabe looked at the signet ring on his left hand, the

Duke of Dale's emblem clear to see in the flickering candlelight. "Because it would not be wise to slight me."

"A sea captain? I always knew you were full of your own self-importance, but really, you are taking your charms too far."

He chuckled. "'Tis true. As a captain I would not be allowed entry, but as the Duke of Dale, there are few in society who would not invite me to their entertainment. In fact, bar you, I believe there would be none."

Gabe allowed the silence to stretch, watched an array of emotions cross Eloise's face. Shock, disbelief, acceptance, and finally anger. He stifled a sigh when the last annoying little sentiment came to the fore.

"You are the long lost Duke of Dale?" She paused, her mouth agape. "What?"

"Is it so hard to comprehend?" Certainly, his mannerisms and polite conversation had at times told of impeccable breeding and upbringing. Had Eloise never once wondered where he came from? What his life was like before the ocean became his home? "I came into the title just over a year ago. My brother loved his horseflesh and ultimately lost his life during a hunt last autumn." He sighed. "You see, I never wanted the title or this life. Only something very special could bring me back to England. Something—" He paused, gaining her eye. "Something other than family duty."

"You're a gentleman?"

The revulsion on her features stabbed at his gut like a knife. "And you're a lady. What's that got to do with anything?"

Curls bounced against her slender shoulders with her rapid head shake of denial. "Men have the liberty to live vicariously and freewill. Women do not. I think you know better than any, I am no lady...not anymore."

TAMARA GILL

"You are my lady, Eloise." Gabe allowed his annoyance to tinge his tone. What was she saying? Because he had lain with her, loved her as any man would have, given the chance, she was no longer acceptable to him?

"A duke cannot marry his whore."

Taking a deep breath, Gabe clasped her hands. "You were my lover, but I never thought of you as my whore." He frowned at her indifference. "Eloise, if I believed you to be someone I could toss aside and forget about, would I be before you now, fighting for your hand and heart."

With a dubious look that stated she was not yet convinced, she pulled from his clasp, walked across the room, and sat. Her forehead crinkled in thought. "Did I not hear something about your abrupt departure from England?"

Probably, he mused. Most of London had. "Something like…?" he asked, not ready to tell her of his sordid past that spanned ocean and land.

"I cannot recall at this very moment, but I'm sure I will." She shook her head. "Does not signify, in any event. You owe me an apology."

"For?"

"Lying to me." She stood and came to stand before him. "A captain? Who turns out to be a duke? Why didn't you tell me?"

Gabe stood and pulled her into his arms. "If you knew who I was, would you have seduced me as you did? If I recall, the knowledge I was a lowborn whelp was a boon for a woman wanting to enjoy and learn the pleasures only a man could give. I doubt you would have allowed me to even kiss you had you known who I was."

Eloise hesitated, clearly fighting her desire for him, before she caught the lapels of his coat. "Even a lowborn

32

whelp was able to capture the heart of a lady. I have missed you."

He lightly brushed her lips with his, inwardly smiled when she moved to deepen the kiss. "And I, you." With every moment, since the day she left, a part of him had been missing. He now realised what it was. His heart.

Gabe lifted her and carried her to a settee—not the widest of seats, but it would suit their needs perfectly well. Eloise lay before him and undulated against his chest. The silk gown splayed about her like a halo of sinful delight. The sensuous ploy made all the blood in his body dive to his nether regions.

Again.

E loise watched Gabe strip off his mask and reveal the handsome face she had grown to love. His eyes swirled like the high seas in a storm when she sat up and helped him remove his domino, allowed her fingers to graze down his chest before stopping at his waist.

"You are not forgiven yet, Gabe."

"No?" He stripped off his shirt and absently threw it on the floor. "Tell me what I must do to please, my lady."

Unable to deny herself, Eloise ran her hand along the taut lines of his chest. Felt every sun-bronzed muscle with wanton abandonment. She swallowed when her gaze noted the hard ridge in his pants, and her own sex thrummed for him to take her there. Touch her. Take her back to the high seas and the many days of decadent love making they enjoyed.

Leaning up, she kissed his chest, allowed her lips to graze one pebbled nipple before tweaking it with her tongue. He tasted so good. Salty like the ocean but mingled with his own sweet flavour. She'd forever savour the taste.

Gabe clasped her neck, holding her against him. She nipped his skin, untied the front-falls of his skin-tight breeches, and watched mesmerized as his straining rod sprung free. His intake of breath made her stomach clench in desire. Eloise met his gaze while she stroked him, let her finger graze the tip and wipe away a drop of his seed as her palm slid over his member and stroked with just the right amount of pressure.

"Have you missed me?" She wrapped one arm about his muscular rear end and pulled him to his knees.

His eyes burned down at her, his ragged breaths all the answer she needed. She bent and licked his essence from the red, swollen head and welcomed the salty tang that settled in her mouth.

"Suck it." Gabe begged, his voice thick with strain.

Eloise slipped her lips over the velvety skin and did as he asked. Using her tongue, she teased every inch of him, sucked and pleased him until they were both rapidly breathing.

"You taste like sin." Eloise flexed her fingers around his taut balls, tight and sitting high against his body. She pulled away slowly, kept eye contact with him, until her lips finally slipped from his manhood.

He came down over her then, his hands frantic against her skirts. Warm air met her sensitised skin when he gathered the material to pool about her waist. He rubbed against her wet folds and mercilessly teased her. She shivered enjoying every moment of time together.

"Gabe," she panted, her nails flexing against the damp muscles covering his back. "What else are you going to do?"

"You want me?" He kissed the sensitive skin beneath her ear and pulled the neck of her gown beneath one breast. Her nipple, exposed to the cool night air, puckered and chilled. Eloise gasped and ran her hands through his silky strands, held him against her as his tongue laved, and his teeth nibbled her breast. She rubbed against him, tempting him to take her. Put her out of this misery. Still, he refused, merely slowed his movements, and tortured her even more.

"Yes, I want you."

He lifted her legs and situated them higher on his waist. "Have you missed me then, my sweet?"

"Yes." She moaned when the tip of his shaft entered her. She bit her lip, her need for him to take her unlike anything she had ever known. Her body felt aflame, her core tingling with the knowledge of what was to come. If only he would hurry. "Please, Gabe."

His eyes darkened before he pushed fully into her, making them one and whole. Eloise sighed against the exquisite sensation of having him in her once again. How could she have thought to live without such pleasure? Live without the man she loved, high or lowborn. She loved him and no one else.

Would no longer live without him.

He rocked into her, the cushions of the settee a comfortable buffer against the hard lines and rock hard man above. With every stroke, he touched the most special part of her soul that sang to him. Called and begged him never to stop.

Eloise flexed her hips, needing him deeper. Harder.

"Do what you just did, again," he gasped, the breath whispering against her ear.

She obeyed, and his rocking turned frantic, brought her all the closer to the pinnacle she climbed. The slap of skin and the smell of sex filled the room. Heedless of their moans and gasps, they made love with a reckless abandon. Gabe's lips remained hard and just as demanding as his rod that slid within her. Eloise cried out and clutched at him, afraid she might shatter entirely, like a mirror dropped from an astounding height. Pleasure thrummed through every muscle, every sinew of her body, left her breathless and boneless as they came.

"Marry me."

Eloise clasped his jaw and met his eyes. "Is that a captain's order?"

"No." He chuckled. "A duke's command."

CHAPTER 7

After taking some time to recover, Eloise and Gabe straightened their clothing and tidied each other up as best they could in a room with neither mirror nor refreshment.

"You have not answered my question, Eloise?"

The steely tone brought Eloise out of her muddled thoughts of what gown she would wear on her wedding day. Where they would live and venture on their honeymoon. She arched a brow at his vacant look. "Really? I thought I had." She walked toward the door and tried to keep the smile from her lips.

A hand clasped about her arm and pulled her around. "No, you did not. And I require one before we leave this room."

She raised her brows at his commanding tone. "Well, even though you lied to me about who you were, left me to sail from Africa to England all alone, and did not have the decency to call on me when you did return to London, I suppose I will."

"I may not have called on you, but I did seek you out as

soon as I could. You should know that if ever I was in the same county as you, I'd never be far from your side."

Her insides melted like Gunter's ices at the heartfelt declaration. Gabe kissed her and fire ignited in her soul. Eloise knew that with one word from her, she could make the wicked thoughts spinning through her mind a reality within moments.

My, she'd turned into a wanton. Not five minutes ago, they had made love with more passion than she had ever thought possible, and here she was once more, thinking of him naked, erect and loving her with his body.

Eloise met Gabe's hungry eyes and knew that with one word from her, she could make her wicked thoughts a reality.

She spied a chair beside the door and pushed Gabe into it. His grin gave away where her gesture had taken his thoughts. With them. On the chair. Having sex. Again. Eloise ran a finger across his shoulder, his superfine coat so different to the tattered, wind roughened shirts he wore at sea. "I don't want to return to the ball yet."

"Neither do I." He pulled her onto his lap and she straddled his legs, lifting her skirts out of the way, as she did so.

Again, the need to have him consumed her. She ripped at his front falls, his cock, hard and heavy in her hand. She came down on him quickly, their lovemaking taking on a whole new dimension. One of urgency that left them both desperate to find fulfilment only the other could bring.

Gabe groaned as she rode him fast, her core clamping down on him, leaving her aroused, and sitting on the crest to ecstasy. "Eloise, how I've missed you. Missed us." His deep baritone vibrated to her core and she climaxed. Cried out as wave after wave of pleasure shot through her body.

Gabe's clasp tightened about her hips, his fingers pinching her skin as he too came a second time.

Her body hummed in sated rapture. With Gabe back in London, the boring life of a lady now seemed far less dull. And she wasn't just any lady, soon she would be Gabe's lady sanctioned by the act of marriage.

She smiled. "I've missed you as well. Dreadfully so."

"I am very glad to hear it," he said.

Gabe kissed her before helping her to stand. Her legs felt wobbly after their interludes and she laughed at their escapades. "Does our betrothal mean you're going to living here in England from now on?"

He nodded. "Yes, but with one stipulation."

"And that is," she asked.

"I would wish we visit Africa at least once a year. Given time, I know you'll love where I made my home, and our children will love the golden sandy beaches that run for miles. I would like to show you all of that."

She had loved what she'd seen of Africa, short as it was. And what Gabe was asking was not at all a great deal of trouble. In fact, yearly holidays sounded perfect. "Perhaps through the English winter months."

He smiled and hugged her to him. "Sounds perfect." He kissed her, seemingly sealing the bargain on their future.

A ruckus from the ballroom brought Eloise back to reality. "We had better return to the ball. The midnight unveiling will happen very soon." Gabe retied her mask and opened the door.

"Good evening, Your Grace."

. . .

G abe looked at the man who stood at the door, and a shiver of unease prickled his skin from the cold, calculating tone.

"Lord Fenshaw, to what do I owe the pleasure?" He walked into the corridor, pulling Eloise along and not allowing her the opportunity to speak or curtsy to the gentleman.

"No pleasure, sir, for I believe you have already had more than enough pleasure for one night." Fenshaw turned toward Eloise and bowed. "Lady Eloise."

Gabe beat back the urge to box the imprudent baron behind the ears. A bright flush swamped Eloise's neck, and Gabe squeezed her hand in unvoiced support.

"Was there something you wished to discuss?" Gabe raised his brows and waited for the words he knew would spill from the gentleman's mouth.

"Of course." Fenshaw paused and smiled at Eloise, a gesture more like a sneer. "I wonder if the woman you have ruined has any idea what a rake and bounder you actually are."

Eloise met his eye but said nothing.

"Rake and bounder no more, Fenshaw," Gabe said.

"Really?" He lifted his chin and looked down his nose. "I beg to differ. In fact, I would lay my entire fortune on the line Lady Eloise would dearly love to hear why I believe this to be true."

"I have no quarrel with you. Now, if you'll excuse us." Gabe took a steadying breath and walked away, knew as soon as he heard Fenshaw's mocking laughter that the man was determined to expose him. Perhaps even forever ruin what he and Eloise had come to feel. He paused and turned back, bringing Eloise to a halt by his side.

"Did you know, Lady Eloise, your esteemed duke

ruined my sister?" Fenshaw paused and strolled to a nearby painting, seemed to take a great interest in the family drawing hanging on the wall.

Eloise met Gabe's eye, then turned to face his nemesis. "Lord Fenshaw, perhaps you ought to speak to His Grace at some other time. Whatever your disagreement, Lord Durham's home is not the place to air such arguments."

"Oh, I disagree. I believe right here and now will do very well." Fenshaw smirked. "Your esteemed duke raped my sister, threw—"

"The sex was consensual. I never raped her." Unable to look at Eloise for fear of her reactions to the man's words, Gabe kept his attention on Fenshaw. True or not, the scandal had near ruined him years ago; no matter, he had not known…

"Threw her out," Fenshaw said. "Without a reference to her name, even when her belly swelled with his babe."

"She was our maid, Eloise, and she came to me. For weeks I pushed her advances away, but eventually I succumbed."

Eloise wrenched her hand from his and stepped away. "Miss Fenshaw was your maid? How is this so?"

He swallowed the dread that rose in his throat and threatened to choke him. "I didn't know she was Fenshaw's sister. And I never forced her. Please believe me."

"Is what this man says true?" Eloise asked, her face stricken. "Did you sleep with your servant and get her pregnant?"

Gabe tried to take her hand again with little luck. "I did, but please, let me explain the full truth."

"Who are you?" She shook her head. "I don't know what to believe."

"He is a bastard and one I have been longing to settle with." Fenshaw stepped toward him and stopped a foot from his face. Eye to eye, nose to nose he said, "Tomorrow at dawn we meet. I will have my day defending my sister's honor, and you, sir, will meet a fitting end for a reprobate."

Gabe turned to Eloise, his heart aching with the pain he'd caused her. She looked lost and confused, and he had hurt her. "Let me explain, it is not as bad as Fenshaw makes out."

"Pistols at dawn," Fenshaw said, giving no quarter on his stance.

"It's illegal to duel," Eloise said, looking at Fenshaw. "You kill a duke and you'll end up hanging on the ropes like the men who rot in Newgate."

Fenshaw shrugged, a mad gleam to his eyes. "If death is what it takes for my sister's honor to be restored, then I will gladly face the consequences. The Duke of Dale wronged our family and will pay dearly for his sins."

At the man's ignorance Gabe's temper snapped. "I never knew she was your sister, and when I did, it was too late to repair the damage I had done."

"That does not make your actions right," Eloise said to him, her brow furrowed. "A servant is someone in your care, a worker who should be protected from harm and treated with respect." A tear slipped free. "I do not know who you are."

Gabe swallowed and pulled forth all the ducal breeding he had in him. "I am Dale. Your betrothed, should I need to remind you."

"I cannot marry you."

Her lip quivered and Gabe fought the urge to wrap her in his arms. Knew any attempt to comfort her would be met with disdain and loathing. "And why is that?"

"You lie," she said. "Lie about everything. About who you are and what you have done. I don't know you at all. And I will not marry you. I'm sorry."

Gabe watched the woman he loved walk down the darkened passage and wondered how the hell he was going to get her back. He turned and looked at Fenshaw, then allowed all the rage he had controlled for the past few minutes to come to the fore. "Pistols at dawn it is. Putney Heath, if you will."

"I will indeed. My second will be in touch." Fenshaw bowed and followed Eloise into the ballroom.

Gabe ran a hand through his hair and cursed. What a mess he'd made of it all, and now, after not even a day in London, and he had lost the only woman he'd ever loved.

Damnation.

CHAPTER 8

"He's a liar and a despoiler of innocent women." Eloise wiped her nose with the back of her hand. Her life was over. To find Gabe again, only to lose him, was too much to bear. How she could ever forgive his indiscretions was unimaginable. "You do not know that." Emma sat beside her. "Listen, I spoke to Bertie at the ball, and from what I could persuade him to tell me, His Grace may not be totally to blame."

Eloise met her friend's consoling gaze and sniffed. "He slept with Lord Fenshaw's sister and left her with child. How can he not be blamed for such roguish behaviour?"

Emma handed her a handkerchief. "Miss Fenshaw's mind was disordered, from what I can gather. She ran away from her brother's estate, and, for some perplexing reason, sought work in the guise of a maid. The duke was a young man then, and although I do not condone his actions toward his staff, perhaps they had formed a tendre of some kind. He is not a vicious or unkind person. Their relationship was a mistake, a youthful folly. Promise, before you act hastily, you will speak to him. Find out what further

44

truths need be told. You love him, and you have a chance at happiness. Do not throw it away."

Eloise stared silently at the unlit marble hearth. "You mentioned she was institutionalized. Do you truly believe she was inflicted with some sort of madness?"

Emma stood and pulled the bell cord for the servants. "I do believe so. I recall Miss Fenshaw during our season, was forever tipping her nose at the ton and its strictures. Forever in some sort of trouble, exhibiting bizarre behaviours. She had a terrible time of it."

The butler entered. "My lady?"

"Tea, Peter, and could you have Cook make up a cold compress please?"

"What's the compress for?" Eloise asked.

"Your eyes." Emma smiled. "We cannot have you speaking to the Duke of Dale looking like a bloated fish that has been for sale too long at the fishmonger."

Eloise touched the swollen skin about her face and knew it would look blotchy and red. Nerves fluttered in her stomach over her impending discussion with the duke. So much rested on his answers, most importantly, their future happiness. Was this past transgression a terrible error, he, as a young man, could not set right? And if he felt no guilt, why flee the country for years? Unfortunately, his actions indicated both shame and guilt. None of it made any sense, and she wished she had stayed to hear him out.

Foolish, hasty, headstrong woman.

"He is to duel tomorrow. I must go. I need to speak to His Grace and convince him to do otherwise. Perhaps now Lord Fenshaw has had some hours to mull things over, he may no longer wish to face his nemesis at dawn."

Emma frowned, directed a maid to place the tea dishes before her, and held out the cold compress. "Not before you hold this to your face for a time. Your eyes are dreadfully red, my dear. Only when I deem you appropriate for company, may you leave."

Eloise lay back with the cooling cloth on her face as directed. "Did anyone ever tell you what a saviour you are? You'll make a good mama, Emma."

"Thank you, dearest." Eloise heard the smile in her voice. "Now, enough sentimental talk, you'll make me cry."

"Very well. I'll not say another word." Eloise buttoned her lips and chuckled.

G abe left for Putney Heath within an hour of leaving the Durham's ball. He wanted to get a feel for the location that might be the place of his demise. The carriage rumbled over the cobbled streets of Mayfair before passing through the more unsavoury locales of London, the stink and rot of its inhabitants prevalent on every street corner.

He frowned at the despicable living conditions and wondered how he could help to improve their lives, should he survive the morning's meeting.

"So it's all over between you and Lady Eloise then?"

Gabe turned away from the dimly lit streets and faced Hamish, his second and midshipman. "I'll tell you tomorrow after I face Fenshaw."

Hamish waved his concerns away. "You're a crack shot. No harm will befall ye."

He could only hope his friend's insight would prove true. Adventure on the high seas, which, many a time, involved armed pillage of English ships, once held his soul enrapt. Made him feel alive, and allowed him to take revenge on a country that had wronged him. But those were the brash exploits of his youth; Gabe found he no longer held such sentiments. Amazed he wasn't dead already from such actions.

Eloise was everything to him, and he would rather die than live without her. "Fenshaw is a good shot, from what I can recall, and he'll be aiming to injure me." Gabe sighed and rubbed his eyes. No, Fenshaw would not wish to injure him, kill him would be closer to the truth.

"Can ye speak to him and talk sense into him?"

He shook his head. "There's no talking sense to him." Gabe's laugh sounded far from humorous. "I tried speaking to him years ago before I left England, and the bastard wouldn't listen. No, I'll have to face him and hope for the best."

Hamish frowned. "What of the duchy should you die? What of ye ship?"

A twinge of guilt settled in Gabe's gut at the thought. He had despised the title and all it involved. Dale, such a proud and honourable name. Second son that he was, he had only brought scandal to the ducal door, tarnishing the family name. Or so his father always believed. Gabe had tried to right the wrong he had caused, but nothing could calm the wrath of his father. Nor could he find Fenshaw's sister to offer for her. Instead, he'd been ordered out of England by an irate father with a demand never to return.

"I should have stayed and fixed this error of judgement years ago. I was a foolish young man who should have known better. Had I tried harder, I could have found Miss Fenshaw. Explained better to father what had happened and what I intended to do to solve the problem." Gabe looked at the box of duelling pistols at his side, his finger absently stroking the wooden casing. "And now it is too late."

"Whatever the future holds, I wish you to know, working under you and being your friend was a privilege.

Rest assured, all will be well. You'll more than likely find when we make the Green Man Inn in an hour or so, Fenshaw is nowhere to be found."

Gabe nodded and returned to looking out the window; the bleakness of the streets matched his mood exactly, but he doubted his friends words. Fenshaw would be there intent on seeking his misbegotten revenge. That there was no doubt.

"He's gone. Already?"

"Yes, Lady Eloise. If you would please enter, I'm sure we can discuss your concerns further, inside." The old butler looked up the street, his eyes darting about, no doubt terrified someone would see her at the dukes door causing strife.

Eloise gave the elderly butler a frantic shake of her head. "No, no. I must go now. I have to reach him before it's too late."

She turned and ran down the front steps.

"To Putney," she called to her driver as she climbed back in her coach. "And please hurry."

She sank back against the plush seat, twisting her hands in her lap. She would be too late, she was sure of it. Already, the night sky had started to give way to the dawn. Had she lost the opportunity to speak to Gabe again, she would never forgive Emma for it. Why didn't her friend wake her when she'd fallen asleep on the settee? Eloise moved to the opposite seat and opened the little window between herself and her driver. "Is this the fastest you can go?"

"Aye, my lady. Any faster and I'm likely to turn us over at the next corner."

With a snap, she shut the portal. Taking a deep breath,

Eloise attempted to calm herself. At this early hour, not many people were on the London streets; they would make it in time. They had to.

The nightmare that had awoken her haunted her mind. Gabe, bleeding and lying dead on the heath…alone. She shut her eyes, not able to bear such a thought. He had wronged, but he was barely a man when he had done so. The fault lie with them both, Gabe and Miss Fenshaw, and he would explain. Eloise was sure.

Should he live to do so…

The carriage rolled around a corner, and she clasped the strap to keep her upright, the steel object in her pocket digging into her thigh.

Fenshaw was mad. Perhaps the affliction that affected his sister ran in his family's blood. Whatever the reason, she did not trust the man to honour the rules of duelling. Her dream had been so vivid and lifelike. No, she would not allow Fenshaw to kill the man she loved.

If anyone was to mete out punishment to Gabe, she deserved the right. He had lied to her. Lied repeatedly, and yet, only to save her from truths that would hurt—had hurt her. She herself was not entirely honest when she'd first met him. Had she not looked at him with longing no virginal maiden should ever know, asked him to teach her to shoot a gun when she could hit a small mark accurately at a hundred yards?

Trivial lies, but lies just the same.

By the time they pulled across from Putney Heath, the birds were singing a tune to the new day. The glow of dawn painted the horizon, dimming her hope of arriving in time.

"Come, we must hurry." Her driver jumped down from the box and ran behind her toward a park. Eloise looked about, not really knowing where she was going. They would have to be around here somewhere.

"'Tis nearly dawn, my lady."

"I know." She inwardly cursed the reminder. Bad enough they were duelling at all. Men and their stupid rules of honor. Whatever was wrong with discussing one's problems like the gentlemen they were supposed to be? Two shots sounded behind a copse of trees just ahead of them. Eloise slid to a stop. Her blood ran cold in her veins, and, picking up her skirts, she ran.

At the sight that beheld her, Eloise, without hesitation, pulled out her flintlock, aimed, and fired at Fenshaw. The man had wounded the duke, and against all rules, was taking aim to shoot him again. Relief poured over her like a balm when her shot sent his lordship's gun flying from his hand, split in two pieces.

Gabe instinctively ducked at the sound of a second gunshot. He turned to see Fenshaw clasping his hand, another pistol shattered at his feet. Confused, he scanned the park, then stilled at the sight of Eloise. Gun still pointed, smoke billowing about her like an avenging angel. At that moment, he knew she was

Indeed a seraph. One who had saved his life. Guilt over Fenshaw's sister or a warped sense of honour had made Gabe fire over Fenshaw's head. He'd planned to accept whatever punishment providence dealt him, but apparently, Fenshaw had not been satisfied with his initial effort and thought to twist fate to meet his own agenda.

Fenshaw's second kicked his friend's gun away and helped the man toward his carriage.

Gabe called after him. "My apologies, Fenshaw. What happened between your sister and me...I made a mistake, and I wish I could repair the damage I did, but I cannot."

Eloise came and stood beside him, her eyes wide with concern at the wound to his arm. "I would have married her," he said and heard a growl of displeasure from Eloise.

Fenshaw halted his retreat. "Bollocks," he said in a menacing tone. "You used her, then left her defenceless. Carrying your child."

"You are wrong. When your sister confessed her condition, I told her I would support her, make her and the child comfortable for the rest of her days. She fled that night. For weeks, I searched but could find no trace of her. Only when my man notified me of her whereabouts and her true identity did I realize what I must do. I came to see you, but you would not admit me. I wrote to you requesting her hand in marriage, but by then, you had shipped her off to an asylum."

"Where you left her to die," Fenshaw said through clenched teeth.

Gabe looked at the man with disgust. Pigheaded bastard. "No, Fenshaw, you left her to die. I tried to right my wrongs. You wouldn't hear of it. Instead, you spread lies about town of my misdemeanour and sullied my name."

"And you left England because of it all." Eloise clasped his arm and frowned. "Oh, Gabe, I'm so sorry I didn't give you a chance to explain."

"I was ordered to leave. My father made it patently obvious he wished never to see me again. He was granted his wish when he died two years ago."

"I'm so sorry." Eloise hugged him, needing to hear his wonderful heart beat beneath his shirt.

He shrugged as he watched Fenshaw climb into his carriage. "You have no reason to apologize."

The doctor, summoned by Gabe's second, waddled over to him, opening his bag as he came. "Shall I have a look at the wound, Your Grace?"

With the help of Eloise, Gabe struggled out of his ruined jacket. The red stain covered most of his left arm, but the injury itself when revealed was only a flesh wound.

The doctor ripped the shirtsleeve away and bandaged his arm. "This should suffice until your return to London. Send for your usual doctor to see to it. Should have a thorough cleaning before it's bandaged again."

"Of course, thank you, doctor." Eloise shook the man's hand.

Noting her paleness, Gabe grimaced, his heart thumping hard against his ribs. He loved her, could see this morning's events had rattled her usual steadfast resolve.

"Very good," the doctor said and bowed. "Good day to you, Your Grace, my lady."

They were silent for a moment before Gabe led Eloise toward his carriage, before he realized he had one more item of business to attend. He turned to his second. "My time on the seas has come to an end, my friend. And so the ship is yours to do with as you please."

Hamish, who was packing up the pistols stilled at his words. "You're giving me the ship?"

Gabe smiled at his friends shock. The man was more than worthy of such a gift, having a steadfast character and generous soul. He didn't know a lot about the fellow, where he came from or how he came to be working for him, but having spent the past two years at sea he knew a great man when he met one, and Hamish Doherty was exactly that. "I am." He looked down at Eloise. "My life is in London now, and it is where I belong. But should you ever need me, you know where I am."

"I don't know what to say," Hamish said.

"No need to say anything, my friend. I wish you well." Gabe helped Eloise up into the carriage. He took a calming breath, the smell of the cool morning air brought his life back into focus. That he was alive was a bonus he had not thought possible only hours before. Now, however, beside the woman he loved, everything fell into place. For the first time in his life, Gabe felt free of scandal. Ready to do justice to his title and to the huge estates he had inherited. "Ride with me back to London?"

She nodded, her dark hair, tied by a loose piece of ribbon, shining in the early sunlight. Gabe shut the door behind them, forgetting his wound, and winced.

Eloise shifted to his side. "Does it pain you?" Her brow furrowed; her bottom lip captured by her teeth. An overwhelming urge to capture her delicious lips overrode all his thoughts of decency.

Gabe tilted her chin and looked into eyes as green as the rainforests of South America. "Kiss me."

"But your arm," she said, sliding a fraction closer.

"Is fine." Gabe bent and took her lips, allowed all he felt for her to come out in the kiss. Hesitant at first, Eloise soon forgot his injury, forgot where they were, who they were and matched his desire. Her tongue stroked his and sent fire shooting through his body.

Lifting her onto his lap, Gabe set about teasing her, giving her pleasure before the tree-lined streets of Mayfair ended their interlude. Not a moment wasted as he supped from her lips, curled his hand about her back, and held her tight against him. Her breasts rubbed his chest, the pebbled peaks straining against her morning gown.

He clasped the strap and held them both upright as the carriage lurched around a corner. Her chuckle brought a smile to his lips.

"We cannot make love here." She chuckled when his hand curved about her breast and kneaded.

"What about sex. Would you be willing to do that here?" Gabe bent his head and took a nipple into his mouth. Allowed his tongue to swirl, his teeth to nibble and tease her into agreement.

Her hands clasped his hair, and Gabe knew she was fighting her own sense of decency.

"My, that feels good."

Gabe set to work on her other breast. "Have you missed me then?"

"You know I have." Eloise squirmed off his lap, turned, and straddled his legs.

Gabe lifted her skirts as she settled about his shaft now straining against his breeches, all but begging for release.

When she reached down and rubbed his engorged cock, Gabe swallowed and tried to pull what was left of his self-control together. Her delicate fingers played to a tune his body knew and remembered well. "I want you, now and always," he said on a gasp when her deft fingers opened his front falls and stroked flesh against flesh.

"I know." The seductive glint in her eyes only confirmed her words. The sex they had enjoyed on the boat was always wild and hot. Gabe could hardly name one place where they hadn't fucked hard and fast but always to the enjoyment of them both.

It seemed nothing had changed. No matter where they were or what they did, pleasure and fulfilment was paramount. And love. Always love.

Eloise rubbed her wet, heated core against his rod, and Gabe hissed in a breath. "Do that again."

She did, and he moaned. He pulled her close and, taking her eager lips, pushed his pants out of the way and released his cock, lifted Eloise, and slid into her heated depths.

"Gabe..."

He nipped her throat, wiggled down the seat, and allowed her to ride him. She was a goddess before him. Hair cascaded over her shoulders, barely hiding the breasts he had freed. The plump globes swayed with their love-making, tempting him like a child in a sweet shop.

"I love making love with you." She ran her hands against his chest, her fingers finding his nipple beneath his shirt and grazing it with her nails.

With barely suppressed excitement, Gabe watched Eloise sit upright and lick two fingers, her eyes wicked with intent. His balls tightened, his cock expanded when she trailed her hand down her body to rest against her sex. A soft moan expelled from her parted lips when she touched herself, stroked the little nubbin he so loved to kiss. Lick. Savour.

The sight of her touching herself was more than he could stand. With a swiftness that surprised him, Gabe flipped her over onto the squabs, lifted her legs about his waist, and took her. Fucked her. Pressed hard against her sex, and watched as her eyes glazed over with wonder and pleasure that ricocheted through them both.

Their gasps and moans echoed throughout the carriage, heedless of the driver who could overhear. Her hot core pulled and contracted about him, draining him of every ounce of life.

"Marry me," he asked at length, leaning over her to watch the woman he loved come back from the exquisite state they always achieved together.

"Why?" Eloise asked, a grin on her succulent lips.

"Because I love you. Need you. Cannot possibly live without you." He leaned down and brushed his lips against hers. "Besides, you saved my life, and now I owe you mine."

Eloise made an agreeable noise at his words and wrapped her arms about his neck. "How could I refuse the captain of my hearts' order?"

"This is no captain's order, my love, but a duke's heartfelt wish."

"Oh, Gabe." She pulled him against her and held him close. "I will marry you, captain, duke, whatever you wish to be. I'll be yours, for now and for always."

He grinned and pushed his now very erect rod against her heat. "I'm having a feeling you need to be mine, again."

Eloise's chuckle rumbled against his chest as she kissed his sweat-streaked skin. "Now would be perfect," she purred, sliding her legs up against his hips, opening for him.

Perfect indeed.

EPILOGUE

E loise walked toward Gabe in the great library of his ancestral home and smiled at the man she would soon call husband. His attire fitted him like a glove, left little to her imagination to what delights sat beneath the superfine coat and breeches.

Before the gathered guests, only the few they wished to share in their special day, they said their marriage vows. Promised each other to a lifetime of love.

It was a perfect morning for a wedding and she couldn't have asked for a better man who stood watching her, his gaze boring into her as if she were the most precious piece of artwork in the room.

Her trip to the wilds of another country with her brother, the heartbreak she'd endured there eased when she'd met Gabe. She was a fortunate woman who would be loved unconditionally for the rest of her life.

She smiled.

. . .

That night Eloise waited for Gabe in his ducal bedroom. The dark wooden bed bore silk curtains that billowed in the fragrant spring air. It made her feel mysterious and seductive. She could hear him talking to his valet as he dressed for bed and she smiled. He had no need for drawers this evening.

The door from the dressing room swung open and Gabe nonchalantly leaned against the threshold. His body was bare from the waist up, and with the flitting moonlight that filtered through the windows, every contour on his well, defined body was hers to admire.

Her body hummed with eagerness to have him close. Over the last few days they'd been separated for the first time since Gabe had landed back in England. And every hour had seemed like a year. "Hello husband."

He pushed away from the door and strolled toward her. The muscles on his abdomen flexed and her mouth dried. He was a sight she was sure she'd never cease looking at.

"Good evening, wife." He crawled over her onto the bed, his hands either side of her face. "Have I told you how beautiful you look today?"

She grinned at his attempt of flattery, which utterly worked wonders on her expectant body. "More times than I can count." She cradled his hips and felt along the taut muscles that ran along his spine. Gabe had a lovely back, strong and straight and gorgeous to watch when he was busy doing manual tasks.

He took her lips and she inwardly sighed. Each stoke of tongue, each sup of her lips left her needy and hot. Within moments the kiss turned scorching, no longer beckoning but demanding, urging her to meet his desire.

Eloise did. She kissed back with all the love, desire and

lust she felt for this man. A man who was so much more than she'd ever expected to have in a husband.

She was a very lucky woman.

Her fingers met the band of his drawers and she pushed them off his hips, using her leg to slide them down to his feet. He chuckled through the kiss before pulling back.

"Is there something you're after, Your Grace?"

She started at the use of her new title then laughed. "Only you. Only ever you."

"I'm glad to hear it." With one swoop, he rolled onto his back and pulled her atop to straddle him. Eloise caught his eye and slowly, slipped her shift off over her head. His heated gaze could scorch skin, she was sure. "Like what you see?"

His hands slid up her waist and flexed over her breasts. His fingers paying homage to her nipples that beaded like hard little sweets just for him. "Very much so."

Gabe went to place her over his jutting cock, but Eloise shook her head. "Not so fast, Duke. I have other ideas for us tonight."

He raised his brows and grinned. "Then please proceed." He placed his hands under his head and watched her.

Eloise felt under the pillow and caught the silk tie she'd hidden there earlier. Pulling it out, she waved it before his face. "Give me your hands."

Gabe made a guttural sound of approval before doing as she asked. She tied them together quickly before lifting them above his head and tying him to the headboard. Her breasts rubbed against his face and she sucked in a startled breath when she felt his tongue lather at one nipple.

Sitting back, she took the opportunity to run her hands

over his chest, his stomach, his jutting cock that sat in wait, hard and heavy in her hands.

"What are you going to do to me?" His arms flexed against her ties and she smiled.

"You should be asking what I'm not going to do." Eloise slid down his body, watched as his eyes widened as her mouth came to sit directly over his cock.

She licked the droplet of come at the end of his penis before suckling the head into her mouth. He groaned, lifting his body a little to push further into her mouth. Wanting to please him as he always pleased her, she clasped his cock in her hand and stroked. With each glide of her fingers he hardened even more, making his thick shaft stand to attention.

Eloise took him fully into her mouth, swirled her tongue about his length as her hand worked him to a frenzy. He groaned, sucked in startled breaths as with each pull and glide of her mouth, she pushed him ever closer to release.

To have such a virile, strong man, squirming in desire, the need she could sense he had for her was the most erotic elixir she'd ever tasted. And tonight was just the start of many more days and night with this man.

Her heart sang with the joy of it.

Sucking harder, she increased her speed and soon had him near the release he craved. Sitting up, she continued to stroke him slower while watching his ragged breathing calm a little.

"What are you doing?"

"Teasing you." She ran her tongue over his penis once more before kissing and nibbling her way up his abdomen. Each taut muscle she kissed, nipped and kissed better before coming to the sensitive spot beneath his ear he loved her kissing most.

"I want to make you burn for me."

She heard the ties flex against the headboard. "I want to fuck you."

His smutty words only made her want him to fuck her as well. But not yet. "Then my plan is working." She placed her mons over his penis and rubbed him against her sex. She was wet and ready, her sex aching with a need to be fulfilled by him. And soon, she promised herself, she would have her wish.

Eloise sat up and without letting him enter her, rubbed his engorged member against her, over and over again she slid against his heat, teased them both to distraction before they were both panting hard, their bodies close to climax but not willing to let go of the delicious ecstasy they always found in each other's arms.

"Fuck me, Eloise."

She smiled and impaled herself on his cock. They moaned in unison as she leaned on his chest and rode him. Pushed them both onward, toward to the divine end they craved. Gabe moaned her name, his arms fighting against his imprisonment. Eloise enjoyed every moment of having him at her mercy. She slowed their lovemaking when necessary and sped it up when she liked. Her body was so close, but her mind wanted to continue the erotic torture.

All through her core she felt her orgasm flow through her. Her body shook as Gabe thrust hard into her sex and pushed her orgasm to peak just as he too found his release. Her eyes fluttered open just as she realized Gabe had freed himself from his bonds.

He rolled her over and pinned her beneath him. "Did you enjoy yourself?"

Her body felt groggy with satisfaction. She chuckled. "I really did. It's enjoyable having you at my mercy. I may have to do that again."

He licked his lips and she inwardly groaned. He was truly too delicious for words. "As long as I can do it to you too."

Hmm. Never had a question been so tempting. "Starting from now?"

"Hell yes. Right now, my little minx. Now put your hands above your head and enjoy."

She did as she was told and settled in for another wondrous orgasm. "I love you," she said, feeling tears well at the fortunate place she now found herself.

"And I you," he replied, before making good on his promise to please her. And please her he did.

Always.

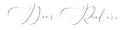

Thank you for taking the time to read *A Captain's Order*! I hope you enjoyed the second book in my Scandalous London series.

I adore my readers, and I'm so thankful for your support with my books. If you're able, I would appreciate an honest review of *A Captain's Order*. As they say, feed an author, leave a review!

If you're interested in book three of my Scandalous London series, *A Marriage Made in Mayfair*, please read on. I have included chapter one for your reading pleasure.

A MARRIAGE MADE IN MAYFAIR

SCANDALOUS LONDON, BOOK 3

Miss Suzanna March wished for one thing: the elusive, rakish charmer, Lord Danning. But after a frightful first season such dreams are impossible. That is until she returns to London, a new woman, and one who will not let the ton's dislike of her stand in her way of gaining what she wants: revenge on the Lord who gave her the cut direct...

. . .

Lord Danning, unbeknown to his peers, is in financial strife and desperate to marry an heiress. Such luck would have it Miss Suzanna March fits all his credentials and seduction in his plan of action. Yes, the woman who returned from Paris is stronger, defiant, and a little argumentative, but it does not stop Lord Danning finding himself in awe and protective of her.

But will Suzanna fall for such pretty words from a charmer? Or will Lord Danning prove to Suzanna and himself that she is more than his ticket out of debtor's prison...

CHAPTER 1

"Are you sure you want to do this, Suzanna?" asked Henry, as he watched her preparations from the doorway.

"Of course. I'm sure. Lord Danning may have frightened me off last season, but he'll not do it again." She shifted her gaze away from her brother as her French maid Celeste pinned a curl to dangle alluringly over her ear.

Henry pushed himself away from the doorframe and strolled over to where she sat in front of her dressing table. He held out his hand and pulled Suzanna to her feet, twirling her slowly as he admired her. "Well, you'll certainly turn heads at the ball. Celeste has worked miracles. I hardly recognize my clumsy, unfashionable little sister."

Suzanna glanced at her reflection—nothing about this sophisticated woman staring back at her resembled the humiliated, heartbroken debutante who ran, not only from a ballroom, but also from the country.

Gone were the orange locks that had hung with no life about her shoulders and the eyebrows that were forever in

TAMARA GILL

need of plucking. Even the little mole above her lip looked delicate and not at all unattractive, as some matrons had once pointed out.

Oh yes, she would draw attention tonight, but if truth be told, there was only one head she really wanted to turn.

"You like this new look, Mademoiselle March?" asked Celeste.

Her eyes sparkled with expectation. "I do." She laughed. "Oh, Celeste, thank you so very much. You have outdone yourself."

And Royce Durnham, Viscount Danning, could grovel at her silk slippers for all she cared. A grin quirked her lips over the thought of seeing one of London's most powerful men clasping her skirts, tears welling in his eyes begging for forgiveness. It would only serve him right, especially after the atrocious set-down bestowed on her last year at her coming out.

Celeste clucked in admonishment. "My profession is so much easier when one has so beautiful a canvas with which to work. I only make improvement with what is before me."

"Too true," Henry stated, kissing his sister's cheek.

Suzanna laughed. Perhaps they were right. For it was *she* who stared back with green eyes so large they seemed to pale the freckles across her nose to insignificance. "I can only hope my deportment has also improved. I was such a calamity last season."

"Was your first season, *oui?*"

"Yes." Suzanna walked over to the window and looked out onto the grounds of her father's London townhouse. "Father having made his money in trade ensured my lack of popularity. I was certainly not fit for some of the mamas of the *ton*." She shrugged away the stinging memory of their rejection. The worst had come from the lofty Lord

68

Danning, a rich, powerful aristocrat, tall with an athletic frame that bespoke of hours in the saddle. He was a gentleman who always dressed in immaculate attire that fitted his body like a kid leather glove, but without the airs of a dandy.

Even the memory of a strong jaw and dark-blue eyes made her belly clench with longing. He was the embodiment of everything one looked for in a husband—until he opened his mouth, spoke, and ruined all such musings.

"Your father was knighted, mademoiselle. Surely, the English aristocracy would not slight your family's humble beginnings. Everyone must start somewhere. *No?*"

"You are right, Celeste, yet perhaps if it had been a more distant relation than my father who made our fortune, the *ton* may have been more favourable toward me. No matter my obscene dowry, they did not welcome me as warmly as some of the other girls."

Henry growled his disapproval. "I'll meet you downstairs, Suzanna, before my temper is unleashed on the *ton's* ideals. Aunt Agnes will be down soon to accompany us, so do not delay." He marched from the room.

"I'll be down shortly." Suzanna sat at her desk and picked up her quill, idly rolling it between her fingers. She was glad she had thought to write to Victoria. Her dearest and best friend would ensure she arrived tonight at the Danning's ball in the company of friends.

"I'll wear the light green silk tonight, Celeste," she said, placing the quill onto the desk. "And Mary," she said to her second maid who fluttered about, tidying the room. "Could you bring my supper up to my bedchamber straightaway? I don't have much time to get ready."

Her maid curtsied and departed. Celeste pulled her gown from the armoire. "There is a small wrinkle, mademoiselle. I will take it downstairs and quickly press it. Your hair and lips, I will repair when you have finished the supper. *Oui?*"

Suzanna smiled. "Thank you. I must admit to being a little excited about going. It has been months since I was in London, and the ball is supposed to be the event of the season."

"And you, mademoiselle, will be the most beautiful of all!"

Suzanna chuckled as the door closed behind her servant. The most beautiful; well, perhaps this once. Maybe if she acted with all the decorum and manners hammered into her over the last few months, a man might magically fall at her feet with an offer of marriage. At one and twenty, marriage was certainly what one ought to think on. Just not with Lord Danning. Not any more, at least.

Hateful cad.

Want to read more? Purchase, A Marriage Made in Mayfair today!

THE WAYWARD WOODVILLES
COMING SOON!

New spicy Regency romance series
Coming February 2022!
Pre-order your copy today!

SERIES BY TAMARA GILL

The Wayward Woodvilles

Royal House of Atharia

League of Unweddable Gentlemen

Kiss the Wallflower

Lords of London

To Marry a Rogue

A Time Traveler's Highland Love

A Stolen Season

Scandalous London

High Seas & High Stakes

Daughters Of The Gods

Stand Alone Books

Defiant Surrender

To Sin with Scandal

Outlaws

ABOUT THE AUTHOR

Tamara is an Australian author who grew up in an old mining town in country South Australia, where her love of history was founded. So much so, she made her darling husband travel to the UK for their honeymoon, where she dragged him from one historical monument and castle to another.

A mother of three, her two little gentlemen in the making, a future lady (she hopes) and a part-time job keep her busy in the real world, but whenever she gets a moment's peace she loves to write romance novels in an array of genres, including regency, medieval and time travel.

www.tamaragill.com
tamaragillauthor@gmail.com

Made in the USA
Monee, IL
04 October 2023